Princess Saves the Kingdom of HONEY

Kathey Morris Mercer

Copyright © 2023 Kathey Morris Mercer
All rights reserved
First Edition

PAGE PUBLISHING
Conneaut Lake, PA

First originally published by Page Publishing 2023

ISBN 979-8-88793-818-9 (pbk)
ISBN 979-8-88793-831-8 (hc)
ISBN 979-8-88793-825-7 (digital)

Printed in the United States of America

To Michael (spouse), Dione and Dr. Wanita (daughters), Corey (son-in-law), and Princess Khori Mikai (granddaughter) for their prayers, love, inspiration, encouragement, and critiques. You all are my greatest fans, and you are always by my side supporting me. I have crazy love for you all.

In memory of my brother, Jimmie, who passed away on August 8, 2023, and who has called me "Cassie" since my starring role in *Cassie's Miracle*. You have always made me feel like a superstar. Thank you for believing in me.

To family and friends, and my godchildren and grandchildren all over the world (America, China, France, Taiwan, Africa, Qatar, Mexico, and Brazil) who have always prayed, loved, encouraged, and supported me down through the years.

1

Princess Khori Mikai grew healthy and strong as days, weeks, months, and years went by. She was kindhearted, caring, and full of love, joy, and laughter.

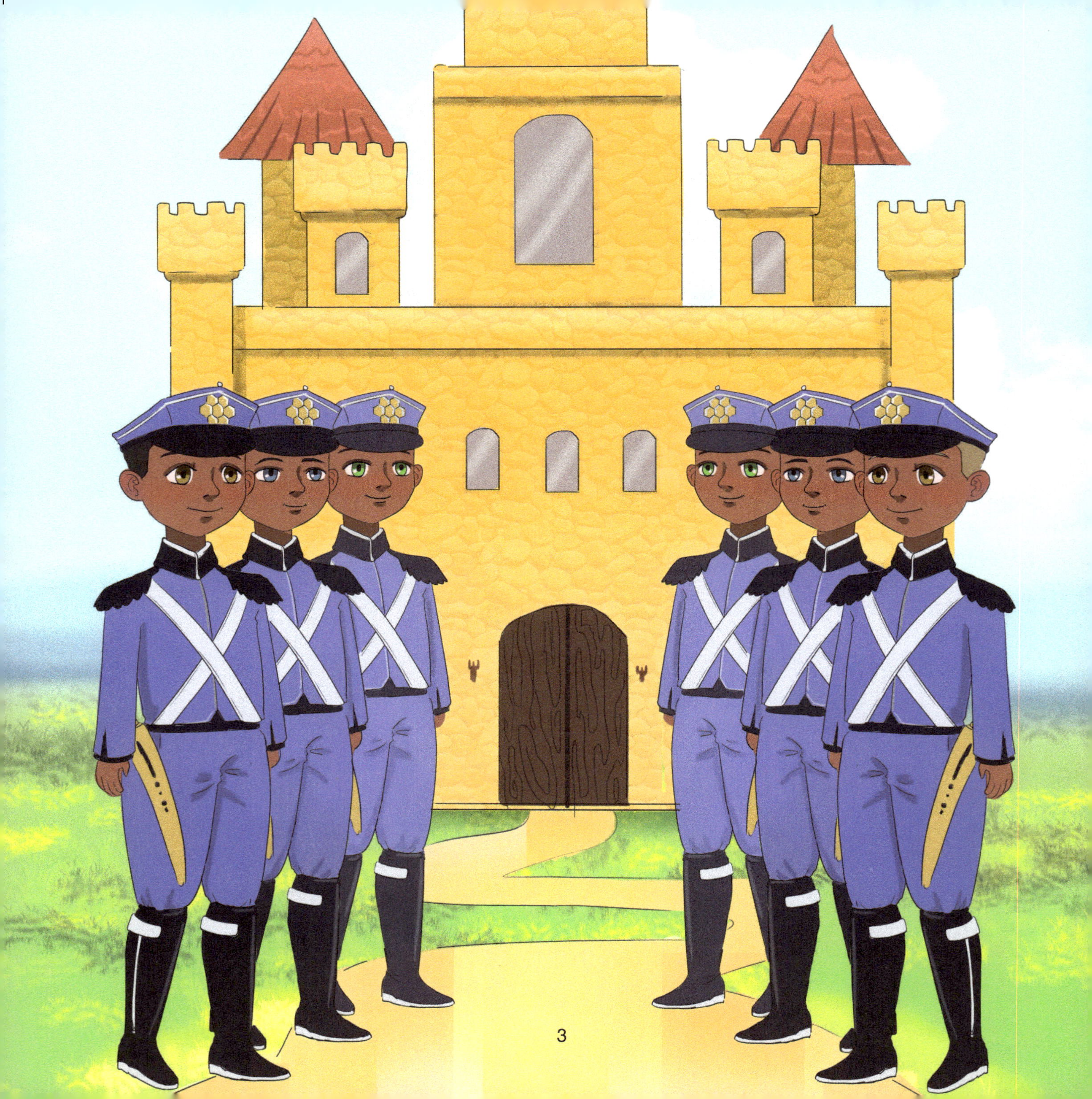

Everyone was eagerly waiting to see what her second power would be, as *foretold* by the prophet. In the meantime, the soldiers were *stationed* on the north, east, south, and west sides of the kingdom.

5

They had fought for years to protect the honeybees, the village people, and the *extravagant* kingdom that many tourists called *paradise*. The king was concerned because the soldiers were growing *weary* and weak from a lack of sleep and *exhaustion*.

7

The soldiers also longed to see the power the princess *possessed* that would save them, and so, they would gather at the castle to sing and pray for a miracle.

9

One day the queen said, "It's such a lovely day, Princess. Would you like to go on a carriage ride through the city?"

The princess replied, "Oh yes, I would."

11

The first stop was the *magnificent* flower garden. There were roses, carnations, daffodils, chrysanthemums, lilies, and so many more; but her favorite ones were the sunflowers.

13

They *toured* the village market, where people bought fresh fruits, vegetables, and meats. They loved the *variety* of delightful desserts and drinks, all freshly made daily with honey.

15

They passed sweet-smelling fountains of honey along the way. They rode on streets of gold that reminded the princess of a story told by the village storyteller about a *glorious* place called heaven.

17

The princess's favorite place was the famous Bee Factory, where the delicious honey was *manufactured*. Until that day, Princess Khori Mikai was unaware of the *violence* from outside forces that threatened the security of the honeybees.

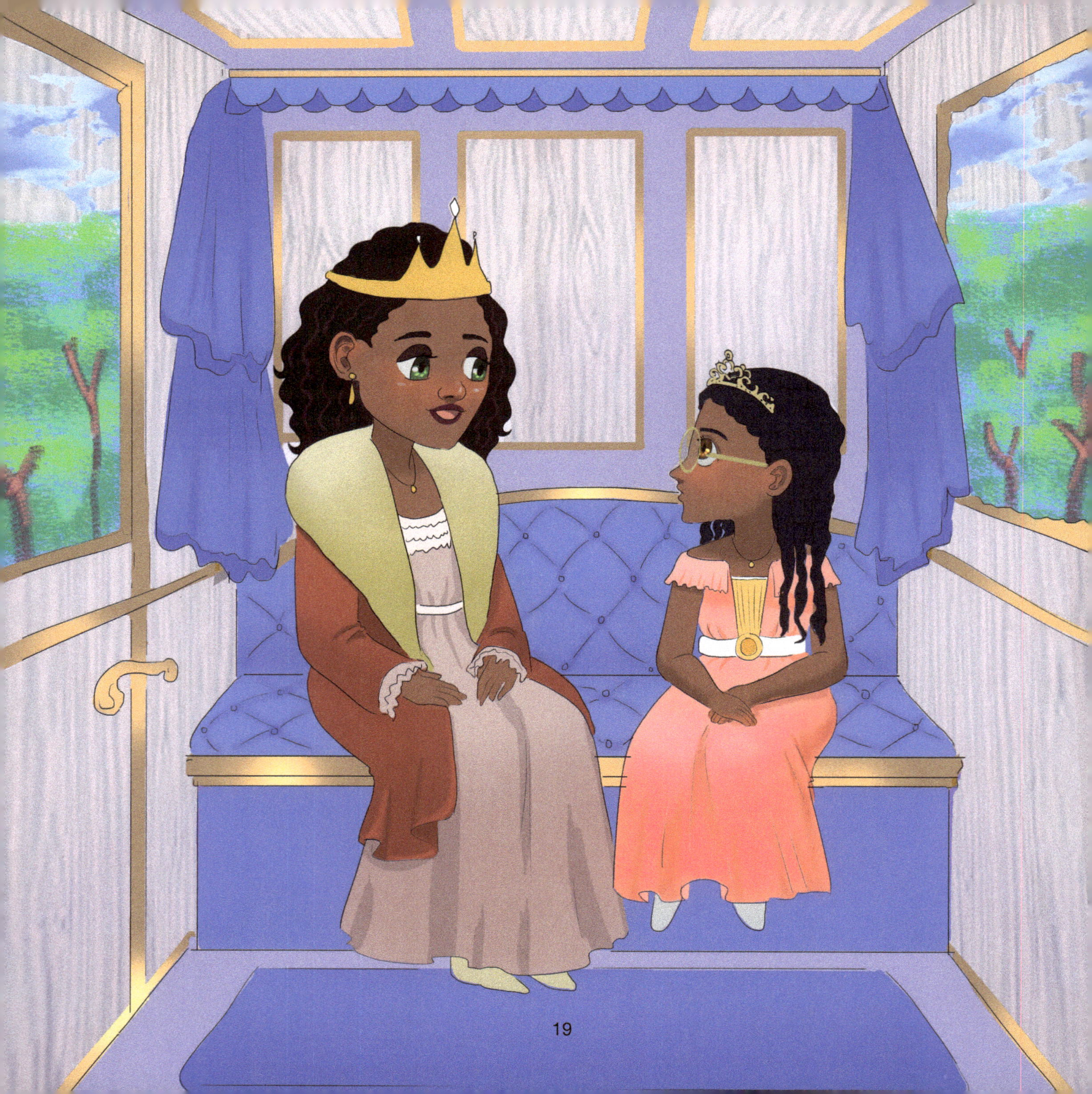

While passing the Bee Factory, the queen told Princess the dreadful news. She explained many bees had been wiped out due to *extreme* weather conditions and *pesticide* usage by the king's enemies.

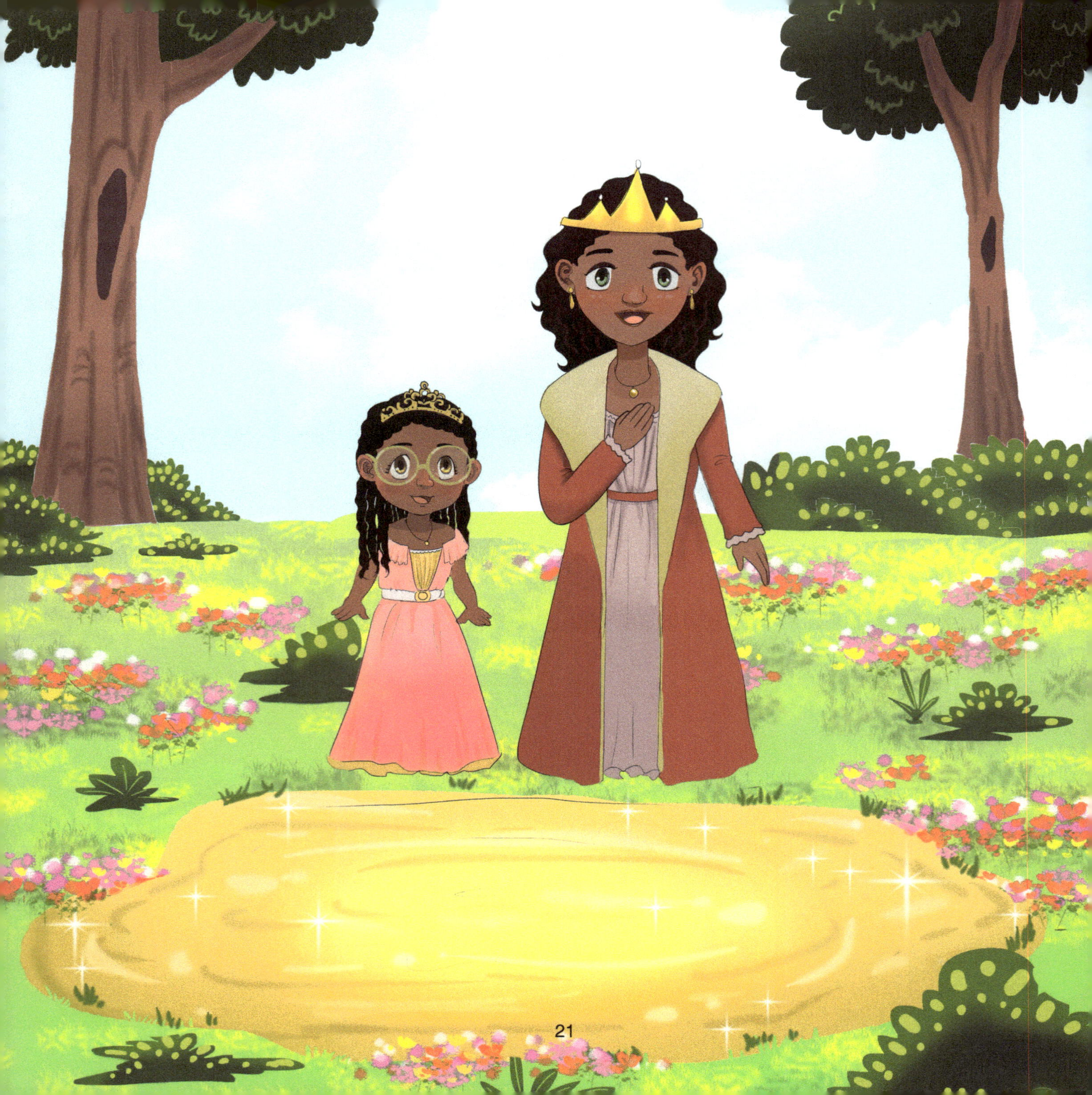

She further explained how outside soldiers from other kingdoms were sneaking in at night, killing hundreds of bees at a time. She said, "The king has done all he can but hasn't found a successful way to keep them out." That made the princess very sad.

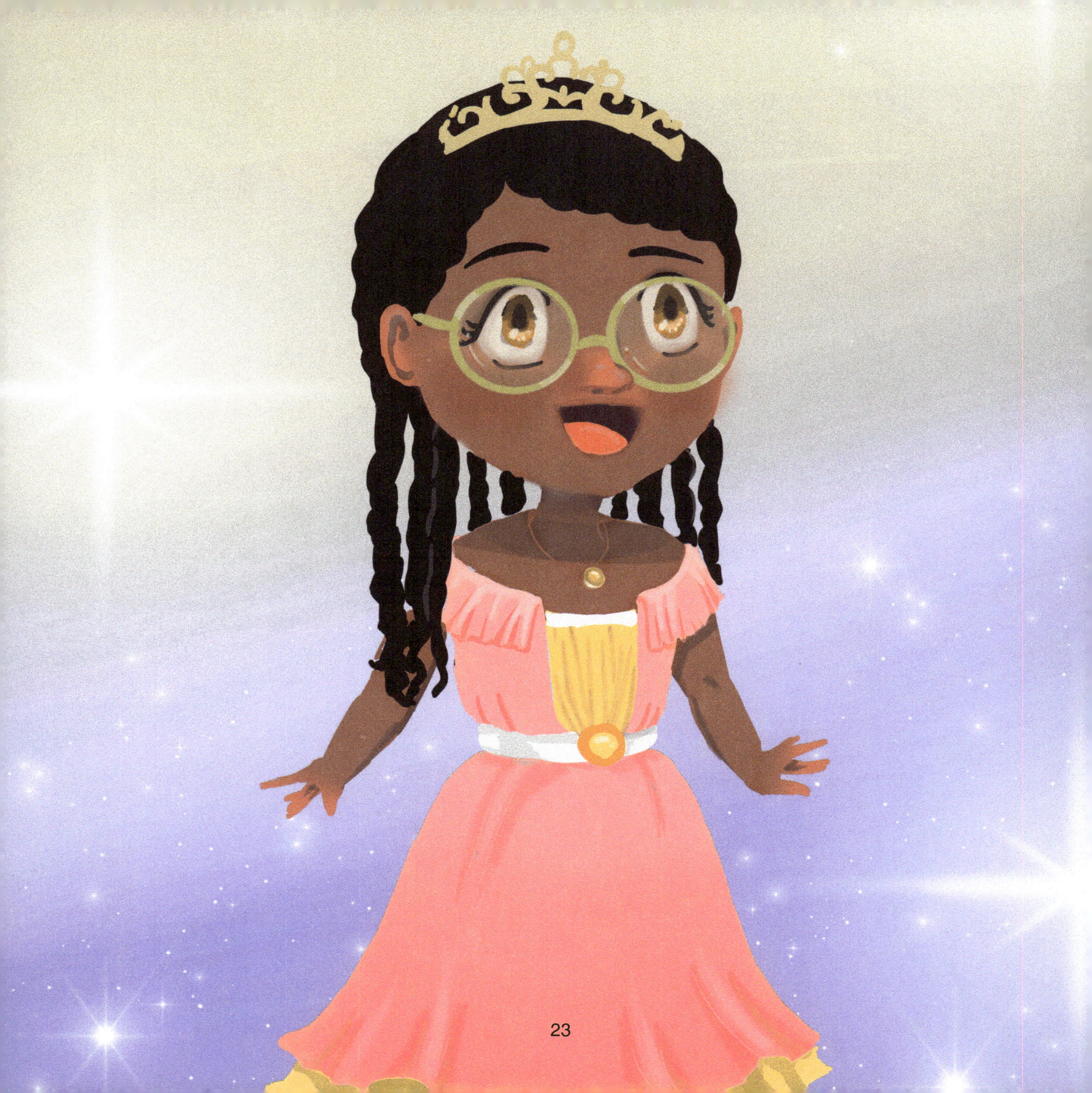

She thought about it and said to the queen, "I know what to do!"

The queen was *ecstatically* happy and said, "What can you do, Princess?"

25

"I can build an *al-ti-tu-di-nous* shield—an impenetrable one that nothing or no one can get through!"

"How will you do that?" asked the queen.

"With my power," Princess Khori Mikai answered.

27

Everyone in the kingdom knew of her first power, the gift of peace. The king had waited *ardently* to see the second power as foretold by the village prophet. When he heard the wonderful news, he *immediately* ordered the soldiers to take the princess to each side of the kingdom.

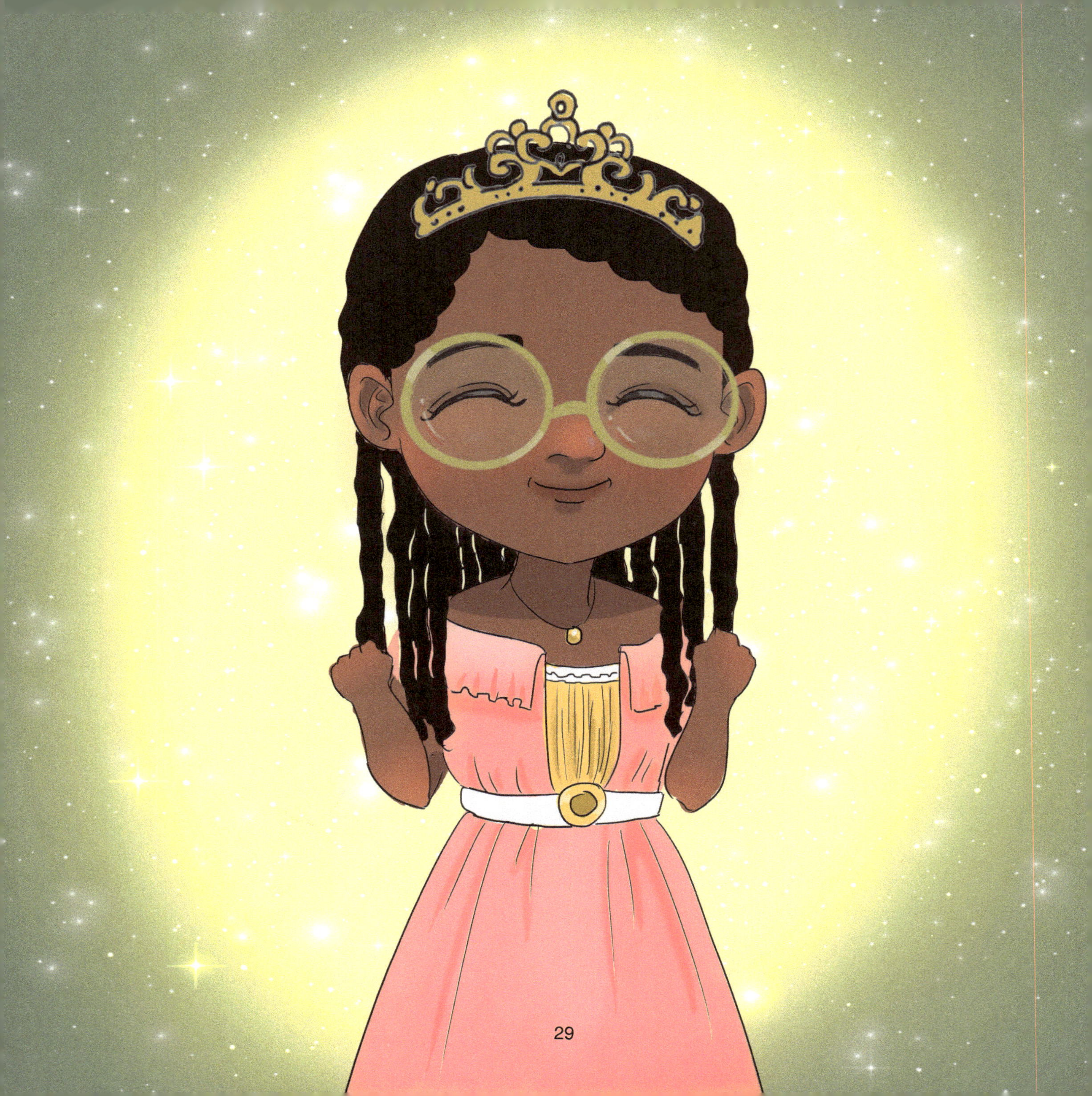

As the princess walked the *perimeter* of the kingdom, she closed her eyes, squeezed her fingers tight into a fist, and an *extraordinary* metal shield appeared.

It was so high you couldn't see the top of it and so strong nothing could *penetrate* it. It was just what the princess had said it would be: *al-ti-tu-di-nous!*

33

The bees were very happy, and the village people cried with joy. Now they would be safe forever.

35

Nothing could *intimidate* the Kingdom of Honey again. Princess Khori Mikai was their hero. And she saved them all.

Word Search

```
H S K I N D H E A R T E D P D P E B
A Q R I M M E D I A T E L Y Y E X O
R K H T E X T R A V A G A N T S H O
D M O P T O U R E D J I K O U T A K
E E O B I I N T I M I D A T E I U X
N X M A N U F A C T U R E D W C S G
T T R N Q L S T A T I O N E D I T F
L R Y N B I F O R E T O L D D D I R
Y E S C B T H R E A T E N S J E O B
M M M A L T I T U D I N O U S A N H
G E R Z U R M A G N I F I C E N T X
M G P E R I M E T E R R B I O G U K
```

Word Find

kindhearted foretold stationed weary extravagant
exhaustion perimeter possessed glorious magnificent
toured manufactured violence extreme pesticide
altitudinous impenetrable variety immediately ardently
ecstatically extraordinary paradise threatens intimidate

Discussion Questions

1. How did the princess grow?
2. What were some of her characteristics?
3. What was everyone waiting to find out about the princess?
4. Why were the soldiers exhausted?
5. What question did the queen ask Princess?
6. Where was their first stop?
7. What could you buy at the village market?
8. What did the streets of gold remind the princess of?
9. Where was the princess's most favorite place of all?
10. What did Princess say she could do to save the bees?

Draw a picture that shows what you liked most about this story.

Fill in the blank with the correct word.

kindhearted   foretold   stationed   weary   exhaustion
manufactured   extreme   altitudinous impenetrable   variety
ardently   extraordinary   paradise   threatens   intimidate

1. She was _____ in England when she met her best friend.
2. As it was _____ the storm caused a great deal of damage.
3. My teacher is friendly and _____.
4. After climbing the mountain, he gave a long _____ sigh.
5. She was pale with _____.
6. He tries to _____ his rivals.
7. My hometown was expecting _____ weather conditions.
8. Both men _____ supported the team.
9. The surrounding countryside was breathtaking and called _____.
10. He had _____ skills.
11. The _____ consumer goods were on demand.
12. There were a _____ of items to choose from.
13. The union _____ to strike if issues are not resolved.
14. The protective vest was_____.
15. The _____ nature of their hike left them exhausted.

Word Find Spelling Activity

1. _____
2. _____
3. _____
4. _____
5. _____
6. _____
7. _____

8. _____
9. _____
10. _____
11. _____
12. _____

13. _____
14. _____
15. _____
16. _____
17. _____
18. _____
19. _____
_____
20. _____
21. _____
22. _____
23. _____
24. _____

25. _____

About the Author

Kathey Morris Mercer is a retired educator born and raised in Jackson, Tennessee. She is passionate about teaching children to read, and that passion was her inspiration for becoming a children's book author. She has received five outstanding teacher awards from Tennessee, Alabama, and Texas, as well as an achievement award from the International Society of Poets. She is a certified life coach, reading specialist, counselor, and public speaker for churches, conferences, colleges, and schools. Kathey and her family live in San Antonio, Texas.

Khori Mikai

Printed in the USA
CPSIA information can be obtained
at www.ICGtesting.com
LVHW070902120324
774241LV00018B/210

9 798887 938189